KU-351-340

I love my daddy

Giles Andreae
& Emma Dodd

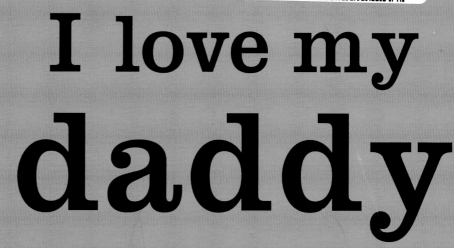

ORCHARD BOOKS

I love my daddy, yes I do,

He's very kind – and funny too.

He teaches loads of things to me,

I think he's clever. So does he!

He lets me clamber on his back,

And we play horsies – click clack clack.

He sings me all his favourite songs,

I love to dance and sing along.

His shoes are very big and brown,

They make me look a real clown!

He lifts me on his shoulders high,

Until I nearly touch the sky.

And when we're playing on the swings,
He does all sorts of silly things.

For treats, when mummy's not at home,

We sometimes watch TV alone!

And when it's time to eat my tea,
He always says, "One bite for me?"

I really love to cuddle him,

And feel the prickles on his chin.

He tucks me safely into bed,

Then tells me stories from his head.

My daddy's such a lovely man,

In fact, I am his BIGGEST fan!